"The Secrets Within"

By Shavar Patrick Jr

Chapter one

"Martin! Martin!" my mom called out to me. I was five years old at the time. I ran downstairs and stood in front of her. "Yes, Ma?"

Her face was pale, her eyes red-rimmed, and I could see tears rolling down her cheeks. "Did you hear about your uncle?" she asked, her voice trembling.

"No," I said, my stomach knotting. "What happened?"

Her tears fell faster as she whispered, "He was murdered."

I felt my heart skip a beat. Even at five years old, I understood what death meant. The weight of her words hit me hard. I was named after my grandpa and my uncle from my mom's side of the family, and now one of them is gone forever.

That night, the house was heavy with grief. My dad came home from work late, as he always did. No one—not even my mom—knew exactly what his job was. When she broke the news to him, his reaction was unreadable. He didn't cry or ask questions; he just stood there, silent and still.

He spoke to no one that night. I could tell the news had shaken him. My dad and Uncle Martin had been close—they had worked together in whatever mysterious job they shared.

Even as a child, I could feel the tension in the air. Something about the way my dad reacted—or didn't react—lingered in the back of my mind, even as I drifted off to sleep. Looking back, I -

realize that moment was the beginning of all the questions I would one day need answers for.

A couple days later my mother and Auntie were planning the funeral date for my uncle Martin. "Can't believe he died so young, he was only 27 years old" my Auntie Amaya said. It was sad to see my family hurting. My uncle was the baby of the family, he was always happy and energetic. (Day of the funeral)
 Church music was playing and the pastor was speaking at the podium. "Martin was a great man, I knew him and his family for a long time, his father was a good friend of mine". I saw how many sad faces there were. It was heartbreaking. I thought it was weird that my father did not want to come to the funeral. Early that morning he said he had to go work and cover someone's shift since they called in sick.

Another strange thing was there was a woman who looked about 25 years old, she was holding a baby in her hands with a child who looked the same age as me. They Were at my uncle's funeral, I knew he didn't have a wife or kids that anyone knew about. That was puzzling. (One year later) I remember we were at a family reunion and it was near a beach called Nickel lake beach. It was a nice beach for us kids to play around at. I encountered a man when I ran off to go and get my beach ball that blew away. The man was slim and very tall. He was at least around 6'9. I said "hello". The man was wearing a black hat with a trench coat with sunglasses. He spoke in this deep raspy voice as if he had strep throat for years. The man whispered in my ear and said "don't you know not to talk to strangers".

Chapter two

"Hey Martin" my mom called. Still frightened by the slim man in the black trench coat, I ran to her and there was the whole family sitting there. "sit" she said, "me and your father have an announcement we want to share with everyone". I wasn't sure what they wanted to announce but I was hoping it wasn't anything bad. "Everyone, I'm pregnant". Everyone was happy and cheering. I had mixed feelings because I truly didn't know what to think at the time. I wasn't focused on that, I was still curious about that strange man that I encountered earlier.

(seven years later) RING RING, that was the bell to go to my next class. I have lunch now. On my way to the lunch room I saw my friends Julian and Andre. We have the same lunch period. "Wadup gang," Andre said. What's up I said. We went to the lunchroom and sat down. For lunch I had a PB & J. My mom made it for me since she didn't have time to cook because she had to drop off my brother at school. The bell rang again. It was time to go home, Andre had asked me if I were coming to hangout with him and Julian. I told him I couldn't because I have some work to do when I get back home. I was riding my bike back home when I spotted a black van sitting across the street from my house. I got a little closer when I saw that same man from the beach in a black trench coat from when I was five years old. The man was looking at my house with binoculars.

My heart was pounding really fast, I didn't understand what was going on, why is this man watching us. I went behind all the way to the passenger side of the car to get a clear look at what he was looking at. To my surprise he was actually spying on my little brother. What is he doing spying on my little brother? Then suddenly the suspicious man turned to me and was staring at me looking deep into my eyes. Then he jumped out of the car and started running towards me. I ran for my life. I wasn't sure what he would do to me if he caught me.

Chapter three

The man was catching up to me. I didn't know what to do. I could hear his footsteps getting closer so I did a sharp turn into some woods. I hid behind a tree, but the man was nowhere to be found. Instead of going home I went to my friend Andre's house. I told him everything that happened. "That's a funny story, I think you should be an author" Andre said. I was frustrated because he thought I was lying. "I'm not lying there was a man in a black van looking at my house". Hours went by, when I went outside it was pitch black. I went back home and saw my uncle Mark from my dads side of the family. "What's up nephew". I said "hi". My mother said that he would be staying with us for a while, because my father had to travel for work.

Me and my uncle Mark didn't really have that connection like me and my uncle Martin did. I couldn't sleep. It was already 2:00 o'clock in the morning. That's when I heard my uncle Mark next door to my room talking on the phone. I went to his door to listen better. "Yeah it's been seven years since the job was done so sad to see him gone so young". Right after that he started to laugh. Wait what does that mean, *seven years since the job was done,* I thought to myself.

Then I remembered, my uncle died seven years ago. Was he really the one that killed my uncle? "No way", I thought to myself. I couldn't believe what I was hearing. Did my uncle Mark kill my uncle Martin?

Chapter four

No it couldn't be, he didn't. I should get some sleep before I think too much into it, even though I have been trying to find out my uncle's killer for a long time. The police tried everything they could to find out what happened, but there was no evidence. (next day) "good morning" mom said. When I walked down stairs I saw a lot of food on the table, and to my surprise my dad was here. " I thought you were out of town". "I got back early", dad said.

Then the tv had the news on it. *"Breaking news there was a robbery at the crescent height bank yesterday night". "The suspects are calvin-".* My dad cut the tv off right before the news reporter could say the names. " the news is depressing". Said my dad. Then suddenly my dad got on his knees in front of my mom, and pulled out a small black box. I saw my mom covering her mouth with her hands in shock. My dad said "Zaria I don't know how much time I have left but I want to spend it with you". Then suddenly he opened the small black box to reveal a huge diamond ring. "Will you marry me?" he said. Mom said "yes" and then they hugged and celebrated. Mom had called everyone in the family to tell them the good news.

(next month) It was the day of the wedding. Everyone Was dressed up, and together as a family. It was nice to see everyone together. But the weird thing is that I saw that same lady with two kids that was at my uncle's funeral. The woman with the kids Were sitting in the back row of the church. I finally built up the courage to go up to the woman and greet her. "Hi, how are you doing today?" I said. The woman had said " I'm fine Martin, how are you?" "I'm-I'm ok," I said , startled. I was wondering how she knew my name. She had said that she was my auntie Amanda. I was confused about how I never met her in my life until now. The conversation got cut off because It was finally time for the wedding. My grandfather was my dad's best man.

Chapter five

The wedding was beautiful, a moment of joy took away all the unanswered questions circling my life for a split second. But even as I watched my mom and dad exchange vows, my mind was racing. Who was this mysterious aunt I'd never met? And why did she bring her kids to my uncle's funeral a decade ago? After the ceremony, everyone moved to the reception hall. The air was filled with laughter, the clinking of glasses, and soft music. I saw the woman from the back row again, sitting quietly at a table near the corner. My curiosity got the better of me, and I approached her again. "Excuse me," I said, standing awkwardly next to her table. "You said you're my aunt? But... how? I've never seen you before."

She looked at me with a faint smile, but her eyes carried a deep sadness. "Martin," she said softly, "there's so much you don't know about your family. Things your parents and uncles kept hidden to protect you." My chest tightened. "Protect me from what?"

Before she could answer, my uncle Mark appeared out of nowhere, placing a firm hand on my shoulder. "Martin, your parents are looking for you," he said, his tone calm but laced with something I couldn't quite place.

"I'll come in a minute," I said, trying to stay polite but determined to get answers.

Mark's grip tightened slightly. "Now," he said firmly.

Reluctantly, I left the table, my mind swirling with questions. Why was my uncle so keen on cutting that conversation short? What didn't he want me to know? That night, I couldn't sleep. My head was filled with fragments of conversations, mysterious connections, and memories I didn't fully understand. I decided to go back downstairs to get some water. As I reached the kitchen, I heard muffled voices coming from the living room.

Peeking around the corner, I saw my dad, uncle Mark, and the woman who called herself my aunt. They were deep in a heated discussion.

"You shouldn't have come," Mark said in a low, almost threatening voice.

"I had no choice," she replied. "He deserves to know the truth. It's about time someone told him what really happened to Martin.

"My dad raised his hands, trying to calm them both down. "This isn't the time or place," he said. "The boy is too young to handle this." I stepped back, my heart racing. They were talking about my uncle Martin again. What truth were they hiding?

Chapter Six

I couldn't stop thinking about the conversation I overheard. They were talking about me. About my uncle Martin. About the truth. My chest felt heavy as I lay awake, staring at the ceiling. I needed answers, and I was done waiting for someone to hand them to me.

The next morning, I decided to confront the woman who called herself my aunt. The house was buzzing with activity as everyone packed up from the wedding celebration, but I caught her alone in the garden, sitting on a bench under a large oak tree.

"Auntie," I began hesitantly, the word feeling foreign in my mouth. "We need to talk."

She looked up at me with that same sad smile. "I figured you'd come back," she said, patting the spot on the bench next to her.

I sat down but stayed on the edge, ready to run if the truth became too much. "What did you mean last night? About the truth? What's everyone hiding from me?"

She sighed, folding her hands in her lap. "Your uncle Martin's death wasn't random, Martin. It was planned."

My heart sank. I had suspected it, but hearing it out loud made it real. "By who?"

Chapter seven

Before the words could leave her mouth, a loud *thud* came from the direction of the house. Startled, we both turned to see Uncle Mark striding toward us, his expression dark and unyielding. "What are you doing here, Amanda?" he asked, his voice low and sharp.

She straightened her back, her calm demeanor cracking ever so slightly. "Just having a chat with my nephew," she said coolly.

"Is that so?" he replied, his eyes narrowing. "Martin, your dad needs you inside. Now."

I didn't move. "I'll go in a minute," I said, my voice firmer than I expected.

Mark's gaze bore into me, a silent warning flickering in his eyes. "I said now."

Amanda stood, her hand brushing against my shoulder. "It's okay, Martin," she said softly. "We'll talk later."

I wanted to argue, to demand answers, but the tension in the air was suffocating. Reluctantly, I got up and walked back toward the house. As I glanced over my shoulder, I saw them locked in a hushed but intense conversation. I strained to hear their words but couldn't make out more than a few snippets.

"You're making a mistake," Amanda said, her voice rising slightly.

"And you're stepping out of line," Mark snapped back.

Inside the house, my dad was sitting at the kitchen table, his face unusually pale. When he saw me, he forced a smile that didn't reach his eyes. "Hey, kiddo. Everything okay?"

I nodded slowly. "Uncle Mark said you needed me."

His smile faltered, and he rubbed the back of his neck. "Yeah, I... just wanted to check in. You've been quiet since the wedding."

"I'm fine," I lied, though my voice betrayed my unease.

Dad leaned forward, his elbows on the table. "You know, sometimes it's better to leave the past in the past," he said carefully.

"What if I don't want to?" I shot back.

His expression hardened for a moment, then softened again. "Life's complicated, Martin. There are things you're not ready to understand yet."

I clenched my fists under the table. "Like what happened to Uncle Martin?"

Dad froze, his jaw tightening. "Where did you hear about that?"

"Does it matter?" I asked, my voice shaking. "Why won't anyone tell me the truth?"

Before he could respond, the back door swung open, and Uncle Mark stormed in. "It's handled," he said brusquely, avoiding my gaze.

"What's handled?" I demanded, standing up.

"Enough, Martin!" Dad said, his voice louder than I'd ever heard it. The room fell silent, the tension palpable.

Uncle Mark turned to him, his expression unreadable. "He's starting to ask questions, calvin. Sooner or later, he's going to find out."

Chapter Eight

The next morning, the house was quieter than usual. Most of the family had already left after the wedding, and the lingering excitement had faded into an uneasy calm. As I came downstairs, I noticed Auntie Amanda was gone. I didn't see her in the kitchen, the garden, or anywhere around the house.

"Where's Aunt Amanda?" I asked Dad as he flipped through the morning paper.

"She left early this morning," he said, not looking up. "Said she had to catch a flight."

I frowned. "She didn't even say goodbye."

Dad shrugged. "She's like that—always moving."

Something about his tone felt dismissive, like he was trying to brush the whole thing aside. But I wasn't ready to let it go. I made my way back upstairs, my thoughts racing.

When I opened my bedroom door, I immediately noticed something out of place. A small envelope lay on my desk, my name written neatly on the front. I picked it up, my hands trembling slightly, and opened it. Inside was a single folded piece of paper.

The note read:

Martin,

I'm sorry for leaving without saying goodbye, but I couldn't stay any longer. The truth is dangerous, and the more time I spend here, the more it puts you at risk.

There's something you need to know: I wasn't just your uncle Martin's friend, I was his wife. We were married in secret because of the lives we lived. The man in the trench coat, the secrets your father and uncle keep... it's all connected. Martin's death wasn't an accident, and neither was our life together.

If you want to understand what really happened to him, you need to start with the box. Ask your father about the wooden box he keeps in his study. It holds the answers you're looking for.

But be careful. There are people watching, and they won't hesitate to silence anyone who gets too close to the truth.

Love,
Aunt Amanda

My heart raced as I read the letter over and over. Aunt Amanda had been married to my uncle? Why didn't anyone in the family know about this? And what was this wooden box she mentioned?

I stuffed the note into my pocket and made my way downstairs, my mind spinning. Dad's study was on the first floor, a room I wasn't usually allowed to enter. I peeked into the living room to make sure no one was around before slipping quietly into the study.

The room was dimly lit, with bookshelves lining the walls and a large wooden desk at the center. I scanned the space, looking for anything that might resemble a wooden box. My eyes landed on a small chest tucked away on a shelf behind the desk.

I walked over and pulled it down, the weight of it surprising me. It was locked, but the lock looked old and worn. My breath hitched as I stared at the envelope. Yellowed with age, it bore my name in a shaky, familiar scrawl: *Martin.* It felt as though my uncle's handwriting was reaching out to me from beyond the grave.

I hesitated, holding it in my trembling hands. Questions buzzed in my mind: Why had this been hidden away? Why was it addressed to me? What could possibly be inside?

Carefully, I slid my finger under the edge of the seal, the paper cracking faintly as I began to open it. My heart raced. I could feel the weight of the answers about to tumble into my lap. Just as I pulled the envelope open a fraction, the door creaked behind me.

Chapter nine

"Martin?"

I jumped, my hand shaking so badly that I dropped the envelope back onto the desk. Whirling around, I saw Max, my little brother standing in the doorway, clutching his stuffed dinosaur. His sleepy eyes blinked at me, full of confusion.

"What are you doing in here?" he asked, his voice soft but curious.

I forced a smile, trying to steady my breathing. "Nothing, Max. Just… looking for something."

Max tilted his head, his gaze drifting to the desk. "Mom says to go to bed."

I exhaled, feeling the tension in my shoulders ease slightly. "Alright, I'll go in a minute. But don't tell Mom I was in here, okay?"

Max hesitated, hugging his dinosaur tightly. "Why? Are you in trouble?"

"No, it's just… our little secret," I said, kneeling to meet his eye level. "Promise?"

He nodded after a moment, still clearly puzzled. "Okay, but you owe me. I want your dessert tomorrow."

"Deal," I said, ruffling his hair.

Max gave me a tiny, mischievous grin before turning and padding back down the hallway, his dinosaur swinging by his side.

As soon as he disappeared, I turned back to the desk. But just as I reached for the envelope again, I heard footsteps echoing from the hallway—adult footsteps this time.

"Martin?" My dad's voice cut through the quiet, sharp and suspicious.

I panicked, shoving the envelope back into the box and slamming it shut. My pulse thundered in my ears as I stepped away from the desk, trying to look nonchalant.

The door opened wider, and my dad stood there, his eyes narrowing as he took in the scene. "What are you doing here?"

"Just… getting a book," I stammered.

"This room is off-limits," he said firmly, stepping closer. "You know that."

I nodded quickly, slipping past him toward the door. "Sorry, Dad. I'll go to bed now."

Chapter ten

The next morning, I could barely focus. My thoughts were consumed by the envelope and the words I hadn't yet read. What could it say? What could my uncle Martin possibly have written to me that my father had gone to such lengths to hide?

Breakfast was a blur. Max chatted about his plans for the day, and Mom fussed over the groceries she needed to pick up. Dad sat quietly at the head of the table, his eyes scanning the newspaper as though nothing were amiss. But I could feel his gaze flicker toward me now and then, sharp and watchful.

I knew I couldn't go back to studying right away. My dad's suspicion had been piqued, and the last thing I wanted was to get caught snooping again. So, I bided my time, pretending to go along with the day as usual. It wasn't until the evening, after Max had gone to bed and my parents were in the living room watching TV, that I saw my chance. Slowly, I crept down the hallway and into the study, closing the door behind me as quietly as I could.

The box was still on the shelf where I'd left it. My heart pounded as I pulled it down and opened it, retrieving the envelope with my name on it. The edges were worn, the ink faint but unmistakable.

I sat down at the desk, my hands trembling as I carefully opened the envelope once more.

But before I could slide the letter out, the sound of soft, hurried footsteps reached my ears. My stomach dropped.

"Martin?"

I barely had time to react before Max appeared in the doorway, his stuffed dinosaur in hand.

"What are you doing?" he whispered, his wide eyes darting between me and the envelope.

"Max, you're supposed to be in bed," I said, my voice barely concealing my frustration.

"I couldn't sleep," he said, stepping inside. "Why are you always here? What's so special about this room?"

I sighed, trying to keep my cool. "It's nothing, Max. Just go back to bed."

But Max shook his head stubbornly, inching closer. "No, I want to know. Is it a secret?"

I groaned inwardly. "Yes, it's a secret. And it's not for you, okay? Please, just go."

Max pouted, clearly not happy with my answer, but he eventually turned and shuffled back toward his room.

Once he was gone, I looked back at the envelope, my fingers itching to pull out the letter. But before I could, I heard footsteps in the hallway again—heavier ones this time.

Panicking, I shoved the envelope back into the box and pushed it onto the shelf.

The study door opened, and there stood my dad, his expression a mix of irritation and suspicion.

"Martin, I thought I told you this room is off-limits," he said, his voice firm.

"I'm sorry," I said quickly, standing up and moving toward the door. "I just… needed some space."

He frowned, his eyes scanning the room as if trying to determine what I'd been up to. "Go to bed. Now."

I didn't argue. I slipped past him and hurried to my room, my heart pounding. Lying in bed, I stared at the ceiling, my mind racing. I'd been interrupted twice now, but I wasn't going to let that stop me. Whatever was in that letter, I was determined to read it—even if it meant waiting for the perfect moment.

Chapter eleven

The next morning, I woke with a renewed determination. The envelope with Uncle Martin's letter felt like a ticking clock. I had to read it, no matter what. Every time I thought about the way Dad had shut me down last night, a fire ignited in my chest. He was hiding something—something big—and I wasn't going to let him keep me in the dark any longer.

The day passed in a blur. I went through the motions, keeping my head low to avoid suspicion. Max was his usual curious self, trailing me with questions about what I'd been doing in the study. I managed to deflect him with promises to play his favorite video game later, but my mind was elsewhere.

By evening, I was ready to make my move. The house settled

into its usual nighttime rhythm: Max tucked in with his stuffed dinosaur, Mom immersed in her nightly soaps, and Dad glued to the news in the living room.

I slipped out of my room and crept down the hall, the faint murmur of the TV masking the sound of my footsteps. The study door loomed ahead, slightly ajar. My pulse quickened as I pushed it open and stepped inside.

The box was right where I'd left it. I pulled it down, careful not to make a sound, and retrieved the envelope with my name on it. My hands trembled as I slid a finger under the seal.

But just as I was about to unfold the letter, the sound of footsteps echoed down the hall. My heart stopped.

The footsteps were soft but purposeful. This wasn't Max, and it definitely wasn't Mom. I barely had time to shove the envelope back into the box and return it to the shelf before the door creaked open.

Dad stood in the doorway, his face unreadable. "Martin," he said, his voice calm but firm, "what are you doing in here?"

I swallowed hard, my mind racing for an excuse. "I... I couldn't sleep," I said. "I just needed a quiet place to think."

He stepped into the room, his eyes scanning the space. "I told you this room is off-limits."

"I know," I said quickly, trying to keep my voice steady. "I'm sorry."

His gaze lingered on me, and for a moment, I thought he was going to press me for answers. But instead, he sighed and gestured toward the door. "Go back to bed. Now."

I didn't argue. As I slipped past him, I could feel his eyes on me, heavy and suspicious.

Lying in bed later that night, I stared at the ceiling, frustration bubbling inside me. Twice now, I'd come so close to uncovering the truth, only to be stopped at the last second.

But I wasn't giving up. Whatever secrets my dad was hiding—whatever was in that letter—I was going to find out. Even if it meant risking everything.

Chapter 12

The days after Aunt Amanda's visit felt strangely normal, yet there was an undercurrent of tension I couldn't quite put my finger on. Dad was more reserved than usual, spending hours in the study. Mom busied herself with housework but seemed distracted, occasionally glancing toward the window as if expecting someone.

That Saturday, while Mom and Dad were caught up in their usual routines, Max came bounding into my room holding a folded piece of paper.

"Martin! Look what I found!" he exclaimed, waving it in the air.

"What is it?" I asked, grabbing the paper from his hand.

"It was in the mailbox," Max said, bouncing on the balls of his feet.

I unfolded the note, expecting some boring flyer or another bill. Instead, the handwriting caught my attention—neat but hurried. It read:

"Martin,
The answers you're looking for aren't in the house. Meet me at the old train station tonight at 8 PM. Come alone."

There was no signature.

I stared at the paper, my heart racing. "Where did you say you found this?"

"In the mailbox," Max repeated. "Is it a secret? It looks like a secret."

"Uh, yeah," I said quickly, folding the note and shoving it into my pocket. "Don't tell Mom or Dad, okay?"

Max grinned. "You owe me. Big time."

That evening, I couldn't focus on anything. The note played over and over in my mind. Who had written it? Was it related to everything that had been happening?

When the clock struck 7:30, I grabbed a jacket and told Mom I was going out for some fresh air. She barely looked up from her book, just telling me to be back before it got too late.

The old train station was only a fifteen-minute walk from our house. It had been abandoned for years, the tracks overgrown with weeds and the building itself crumbling. The place was eerie, especially at night, but I was too curious—and maybe a little reckless—to care.

I arrived just before 8 PM, my breath visible in the chilly air. The station was empty, its broken windows staring back at me like hollow eyes. For a moment, I wondered if I'd been tricked.

But then I saw a figure step out of the shadows.

It was a woman, her face partially obscured by the hood of her jacket. She looked around cautiously before speaking. "Martin?"

"Yes," I said, my voice steady despite the nerves bubbling in my stomach. "Who are you?"

She pulled back her hood, revealing a face that was vaguely familiar. "My name is Elena. I used to work with your uncle."

"My uncle Martin?" I asked, surprised.

"Yes," she said. "I know you've been digging into things. I'm here to warn you—what you're looking for isn't as simple as you think."

"What do you mean?" I pressed, taking a step closer.

"Your uncle was involved in something… complicated," Elena said carefully. "And your dad knows more than he's letting on."

"Why are you telling me this?"

"Because," she said, her voice dropping to a whisper, "you deserve to know the truth. But if you keep poking around the way you've been doing, you're going to attract attention. The kind you don't want."

I frowned. "What kind of attention?"

"The kind that makes people disappear," she said grimly.

A chill ran down my spine. "So what am I supposed to do?"

"For now, keep your head down," she said. "When the time is right, I'll reach out to you again. Until then, be careful who you trust—even in your own family."

With that, she turned and disappeared into the night, leaving me standing there with more questions than answers.

As I walked home, her words echoed in my mind. *Be careful who you trust.*

I had no idea what I was getting into, but one thing was clear—my family was hiding something, and I was determined to find out what it was.

Chapter 13

The feeling hit me as I walked home from school. A sensation of being watched, the kind that prickles the back of your neck and makes your steps quicken even if you don't know why.

I glanced over my shoulder casually, trying not to seem obvious. At first, I saw nothing—just the usual people milling about, cars driving by. But then I spotted him, standing at the far end of the block.

The man in the trench coat.

It was him. The same figure I'd seen when I was five. Even though it had been years, I remembered him vividly. The wide-brimmed hat, the way the shadow of the brim obscured his face, the stiff, almost mechanical way he held himself.

For years, I'd convinced myself he wasn't real, that he was some trick of a young mind processing grief and confusion. But now he was here, standing in the same unmistakable coat, watching me.

My heart raced as I turned the corner, quickening my pace. I told myself not to run. Running would only make it worse. Instead, I darted into a small grocery store on the corner and lingered near the shelves, pretending to browse.

Peeking out the store window, I saw him walk past. His steps were deliberate, unhurried. He didn't even glance at the store.

"Can I help you with something?" the cashier asked, startling me.

"No, I'm good," I replied quickly, grabbing a pack of gum to avoid looking suspicious. After paying, I stepped out cautiously, looking both ways.

He was gone.

By the time I got home, my nerves were still raw. The house was quiet—Dad was working late, Mom was busy in the kitchen, and Max was glued to the TV. I slipped into my room, locking the door behind me.

Sitting at my desk, I pulled out my notebook and opened it to the page where I'd been tracking everything:

1. Uncle Martin's death wasn't an accident.
2. Dad knows more than he's letting on.
3. The man in the trench coat was there when I was five—and now he's back.

I stared at the list, my pen hovering over the paper. Was it a coincidence? Or had he been following me all along? And if so, why?

Suddenly, a memory bubbled to the surface—an image of the man standing outside the house the night we found out about Uncle Martin's death. He hadn't approached or said anything. He'd just… stood there, as if waiting for something.

What if he wasn't waiting? What if he was watching?

A knock on my door made me jump.

"Martin? Dinner's ready," Mom called.

"Coming," I said, stuffing the notebook into my drawer.

At the table, I tried to act normal, but I couldn't shake the feeling that he was still out there, lurking in the shadows.

After dinner, I made an excuse to take the trash out. As I stepped into the backyard, I scanned the street. It was empty, quiet except for the hum of distant traffic.

But as I turned to go back inside, I froze.

At the far end of the street, near the lamppost, he stood again. The man in the trench coat.

This time, he wasn't just watching. He tilted his head slightly, as if acknowledging me.

My pulse thundered in my ears as I stumbled back into the house, locking the door behind me.

Who was he? What did he want?

And most importantly, why did he always show up whenever Uncle Martin's name was brought to light?

Chapter 14

I couldn't sleep that night. Every time I closed my eyes, I saw the man in the trench coat standing beneath the streetlight, his silhouette etched against the dim glow. What was he doing? Why had he come back now, after all these years?

By morning, I felt no closer to answers. Over breakfast, Max chattered away about a school project, and Mom reminded me to clean my room. Dad barely looked up from his coffee, his expression distant. I wondered if he had noticed anything unusual—or if he even cared.

On my walk to school, I couldn't stop myself from scanning the streets. Every shadow seemed too sharp, every figure too familiar. I wanted to believe it was all in my head, but I couldn't shake the feeling that I wasn't alone.

At school, I was distracted. I could barely pay attention in class, my mind looping back to the man. During lunch, I sat with my friends but barely participated in the conversation. My best friend, Julian, finally nudged me.

"Hey, Earth to Martin. What's up with you?"

"Nothing," I said too quickly.

Julian raised an eyebrow. "You're a terrible liar. Spill."

I hesitated. Julian was my closest friend, but how could I explain something like this without sounding crazy?

"It's just… family stuff," I said finally. It wasn't a lie, technically.

Julian studied me for a moment, then nodded. "Alright. But if you need to talk, I'm here."

"Thanks," I mumbled.

After school, I lingered in the library, hoping to find something—anything—that might help me understand what was going on. I searched for books on private investigators, strange men in trench coats, even urban legends. But nothing seemed to fit.

As the sun dipped low in the sky, I decided to head home. The streets were quieter than usual, the fading light casting long shadows. I walked quickly, keeping my head down, but halfway home, I felt it again—that prickling sensation of being watched.

I turned slowly, my heart pounding.

There he was. The man in the trench coat, standing across the street.

This time, I didn't look away. I stood frozen, staring at him, hoping to catch a glimpse of his face. But the shadows of his hat and the evening light obscured it, just as they always had.

Summoning all my courage, I took a step toward him. "Who are you?" I called out. My voice wavered, but I forced myself to stand tall. "What do you want?"

He didn't move. He didn't speak.

I took another step, then another, crossing the street. But as I got closer, a car drove past, momentarily blocking my view.

When it passed, he was gone.

I stood there, staring at the empty spot where he'd been. My chest felt tight, my mind racing. How did he vanish so quickly? Was he real, or was I losing it?

When I got home, I went straight to my room, locking the door behind me. Pulling out my notebook, I scribbled down everything:

- He was watching me again.
- He's always just out of reach.
- Why does he disappear?
- What does he want from me?

I stared at the page, my pen hovering over the last line. For a fleeting moment, I considered telling my dad. But what would I say? *Hey, Dad, remember that mysterious guy from when I was five? He's back!*

No. This was something I had to figure out on my own.

That night, I barely slept. When I finally did drift off, my dreams were filled with shadows and the sound of footsteps echoing in the dark.

By the time I woke up, I was more determined than ever. Whoever the man was, he wasn't going to keep me in the dark any longer.

Chapter 15

The days passed in a blur. Each one felt like a repeating loop, where I woke up, went to school, and came back home to stare at the shadows, hoping they wouldn't shift into the form of the man in the trench coat. I couldn't shake the nagging feeling that I was being pulled into something much bigger than I could understand.

One afternoon, I decided to visit the local library. Maybe there was something in the archives I hadn't seen before, a clue that would explain why the man had been following me all these years. As I walked through the rows of books, the smell of dust and old paper filled the air. It was comforting, in a way, like I had a chance to lose myself in something that wasn't quite so terrifying.

I found a secluded corner, away from the main shelves. I'd been coming to this library for years, but I never ventured into the old history section. Today, something pulled me toward it. I reached up to pull a dusty book off the shelf, its spine creaking as I opened it.

The book was about local legends and strange occurrences in the town's history. As I skimmed through the pages, one section caught my eye. It was about sightings of a mysterious figure in a long coat that had been reported by several people over the years. The description matched the man I'd seen so many times—tall, thin, with a long, dark coat and a wide-brimmed hat.

The passage read:

"In the years following the Great Fire of 1933, a figure began appearing around the town at night. Descriptions of him vary, but one thing is consistent—he wears a long, dark coat and is always seen near the edges of the town, as if watching. There are whispers of him being tied to a family in the area, a lineage whose secrets are buried deep. Some believe he is a guardian, others a harbinger of something darker. His presence is always marked by a deep, unsettling silence, and those who encounter him report a strange feeling of déjà vu, as if they've seen him before, but can never quite place where."

My breath caught in my throat. It was the man. This book, published decades ago, had mentioned him. But why? Why was this figure associated with my family, and why had he been following me all this time?

I turned the page, desperate to find more information, but the next paragraph was torn. The edges were ragged, as though someone had ripped it out on purpose.

Frustration rose within me. I slammed the book shut and glanced around the library, hoping no one had seen me. My heart was racing, and for a moment, I wondered if I should just leave—if I was digging into something that I wasn't ready to understand.

But I couldn't stop now. I had to know who he was, and why he kept showing up.

As I walked out of the library, the weight of the book in my bag seemed to grow heavier with each step. I couldn't shake the feeling that I was being watched, just like I had been since I first saw the man. Was it a coincidence that he appeared in my life around the same time the book mentioned him? Was my family connected to this strange figure, as the book hinted?

That night, I sat at my desk, staring at the pages I'd copied from the book. The silence in my room was deafening. Outside, the wind howled, rattling the window panes. I couldn't help but feel that the answers were just beyond my reach, like a puzzle I was close to solving but couldn't quite finish.

I glanced at the clock. It was nearly midnight. I needed sleep, but my mind wouldn't let me rest. Instead, I gathered my courage and made a decision: tomorrow, I would ask my father about the man. I didn't care if he got angry. I needed answers, and I wasn't going to stop until I got them.

Just as I stood up to leave my room, I heard a soft knock on the door.

"Martin?" It was my dad's voice. He sounded tired, but there was something else in his tone—a hint of concern. "Can we talk?"

My heart skipped. Had he found out? Did he know I was snooping around the old library?

I opened the door slowly. My dad stood there, his face drawn with a seriousness I'd never seen before.

"Yeah, Dad? What's up?" I asked, trying to sound calm.

He looked at me for a long moment before speaking. "You've been quiet lately. Is everything okay?"

I hesitated, the weight of everything I had discovered pressing on my chest. I almost told him. I almost said everything. But something stopped me—something about the way he was looking at me, like he was waiting for me to make the first move. I wasn't sure if he would tell me the truth, even if I asked.

"Yeah," I said finally. "Everything's fine."

He nodded, but I could see the doubt in his eyes. "Alright. Just remember, if you need anything, I'm here." He gave me a brief smile before turning away.

As he walked down the hallway, I closed the door behind me and let out a shaky breath. Whatever the man in the trench coat was, whatever connection my family had to him, I wasn't going to stop searching. But now, I was more certain than ever—my father was hiding something from me, and the truth was closer than I realized.

Chapter 16

It started like any other evening, with the hum of the TV in the living room blending into the faint clatter of dishes from the kitchen. I sat on the couch, half-watching some crime drama while Max played on the floor with his dinosaur figurines. Mom was busy folding laundry, and Dad was perched in his armchair, a mug of coffee in hand.

That's when the news bulletin interrupted the program.

"Breaking news," the anchor said, her tone somber. "Police have arrested a suspect in connection with the recent string of bank robberies across the county. Authorities say—"

Before I could catch more details, Dad shot up from his chair and grabbed the remote.

"Don't you boys have homework to finish?" he said hastily, turning off the TV before any of us could respond. His voice was firm, but there was something else there—something tense.

I didn't think much of it at the time, brushing it off as just another one of Dad's quirks. But now, sitting in my room with the weight of the past few days pressing on my chest, I couldn't ignore it.

That night came rushing back to me. I remembered how Dad had avoided eye contact, how his fingers had trembled slightly as he set the remote down. And then there was the news itself—something about suspects, a robbery, and surveillance footage.

The puzzle pieces were falling into place, but I didn't want to believe it. My dad—the man who fixed my bike, who taught me how to throw a baseball, who seemed to carry the weight of the world on his shoulders—was now a suspect in something as serious as bank robbery?

A loud knock on the front door shattered my thoughts.

I bolted upright, my heart racing as I listened to the heavy footsteps and muffled voices downstairs.

"Mrs. Jensen," a firm voice said, "we have a warrant for Calvin Jensen's arrest. Please step aside."

I stumbled to my bedroom door and peeked out into the hallway. Max's door creaked open, and his small face appeared, his eyes wide with confusion and fear.

"What's happening?" he whispered.

"I—I don't know," I whispered back.

We crept down the stairs together, staying out of sight. From our hiding spot, I saw two police officers standing in the foyer. Dad stood in front of them, his hands raised slightly, his face calm but pale.

"Calvin Jensen, you are under arrest for your involvement in the Crescent Heights Bank robbery," one of the officers said, stepping forward with handcuffs.

"Dad?" I couldn't stop myself from calling out.

Dad turned his head slightly, his eyes meeting mine. His expression was unreadable, a mix of regret and resignation. "Martin, Max, go back to your rooms," Mom said sharply, her voice trembling.

"Wait," I blurted out, stepping into view. "This can't be right. He didn't do anything!"

"Martin, listen to your mother," Dad said, his voice steady but firm.

The officers placed the handcuffs on him and began leading him out of the house. Mom stood frozen, her hands clasped tightly in front of her.

"Mom, what's going on?" I demanded.

She didn't answer. Her gaze was fixed on the door as it closed behind Dad and the officers.

As the police car's sirens faded into the distance, silence fell over the house.

Later that night, I sat on the edge of my bed, trying to process everything. The pieces clicked together—the tense reaction to the news, the sudden mood shifts, the long hours at work that no one ever questioned.

I opened my laptop and searched for articles about the robbery. Sure enough, there it was: **"Suspects Sought in Connection with Crescent Heights Bank Heist."** The accompanying images showed blurry figures in masks, but something about the way one of them stood, the slight slouch of his shoulders—it felt eerily familiar. I closed the laptop, my chest tightening.The man I thought I knew so well now seemed like a stranger. And for the first time in my life, I wasn't sure if I could trust my dad—or the truth about our family.

Chapter 17

After Dad's arrest, the house felt like it had been hollowed out. Mom floated through her days in a daze, Max clung to his stuffed dinosaur more than ever, and I... I couldn't stop thinking.

The robbery was shocking enough, but it felt like just another puzzle piece in a larger, darker picture—one that started years ago with my Uncle Martin's murder. The more I thought about it, the more I couldn't shake the feeling that the two were connected.

I needed answers.

I started with the journal I'd found in the study, the one I'd barely had a chance to skim. Late that night, after everyone else was asleep, I slipped into the study and retrieved the box again. This time, I took it back to my room, locking the door behind me.

The entries were just as cryptic as before.

- *March 15: The job's done, but I can't shake the guilt. I hope this keeps the family safe.*
- *April 2: Amaya keeps asking questions. She won't stop until she knows the truth. I don't know how much longer we can keep this hidden.*
- *July 27: Martin didn't deserve this. But it was him or us.*

I stared at that last line, my heart racing. "Him or us." What did that mean? And what could my dad have done that made him feel guilty enough to write about it?

Suddenly, a memory surfaced.

I was five years old, sitting on the living room floor while my dad and Uncle Martin talked in the kitchen. I couldn't remember all the details of their conversation, but one line from Uncle Martin came back to me as clear as day: *"This deal is too dangerous, Mike. If it goes wrong, we're all done for."*

I'd been too young to understand at the time, but now it felt like a clue.

The next morning, I tried to piece together what I knew. Dad had been arrested for a robbery, but he and Uncle Martin had been involved in something shady years before. And there was still the man in the trench coat—the one I'd seen when I was five and again just a few days ago.

Was he the missing link?

I decided to start digging. First, I went back to the journal and focused on the entries from around the time of Uncle Martin's death. The dates were close—too close. And the entry about Amaya asking questions stood out.

I thought about Aunt Amaya, how she'd always seemed on edge after Uncle Martin's death. Had she known something? Had she been trying to find out the truth?

The pieces swirled in my mind, tantalizingly close to forming a picture.

Then I remembered the news Dad had turned off so abruptly the night of his arrest. I searched online, finding articles about the Crescent Heights Bank robbery. It mentioned multiple suspects and hinted at connections to an older unsolved case—a case involving stolen money that had never been recovered.

Could that have been the "deal" Uncle Martin warned Dad about?

The more I dug, the more tangled the web became. The murder, the robbery, the mysterious man in the trench coat—they were all connected. I was sure of it.

But the answers I needed weren't in the articles or the journal. They were with the people involved. And one of those people was sitting in a jail cell.

If I wanted the truth, I was going to have to face my father—and ask him the questions no one else dared to.

Chapter 18

I sat cross-legged on my bedroom floor, surrounded by a mess of old newspapers, photocopied police reports, and Uncle Martin's journal. My heart pounded in my chest as I pieced together the puzzle. I could feel it—I was so close to the truth.

The journal entry from just days before Uncle Martin's death was burned into my mind:

"I told Calvin this deal was bad news. If it goes south, they'll come after me first. Maybe I should come clean."

Calvin. My dad.

I had spent days questioning everything I thought I knew about my father. And now, I couldn't ignore the sinking feeling in my gut. My dad had to be involved somehow. But how? What was this "deal" Uncle Martin had mentioned?

The name **Victor Kane** kept popping up in the investigation—a local mobster with connections to the city's criminal underworld. Uncle Martin's warnings about "the deal" and his cryptic notes about threats made me wonder if Kane had been involved in something darker.

I opened my laptop and started searching for any information I could find on Victor Kane. After an hour of digging through old police reports and articles, I found something—a lead. A warehouse near the old docks, a place known to be one of Kane's safe houses.

I arrived at the warehouse just as the sun was setting, the last light of day filtering through the broken windows. The place felt abandoned, but I wasn't fooling myself. I had to be careful.

The smell of saltwater and rust hit me as soon as I stepped inside, and I pulled my jacket tighter around me, trying to shake off the uneasy feeling crawling up my spine. Dust covered every surface, and the place looked like it hadn't been touched in years.

I crept through the dark, flashlight in hand, scanning the room for anything useful. And then I saw it—an old filing cabinet tucked in the corner, its drawers half-open. My pulse quickened. I approached slowly, half-expecting someone to jump out of the shadows.

But no one did.

I opened the drawer, and there it was—a dusty folder, shoved to the back. The label read **Victor Kane** in bold black ink. I pulled it out, hands shaking, and flipped it open. Inside were a series of documents detailing financial transactions between Kane and several local businesses—including one owned by my dad.

"This is it," I whispered to myself.

But then, something caught my eye. Another envelope, wedged between the papers, with my uncle's name scrawled across the front. My heart nearly stopped.

I ripped it open, desperate to see what was inside. The letter was brief, but it was enough to make my blood run cold. It was written in Uncle Martin's shaky handwriting:

"Victor's threatening me. He knows about the ledger, but I won't give it up. It's my only insurance. Calvin keeps saying we can handle this, but I don't trust him anymore. If something happens to me, the ledger is hidden where we made the deal."

I stood there frozen, the letter trembling in my hands. What deal? And what ledger was he talking about?

My mind raced. If Uncle Martin had hidden something, something big enough to threaten his life, it was out there somewhere. And it could be the key to everything—the robbery, my dad's arrest, and maybe even his involvement in Uncle Martin's death.

But just as I was about to gather my thoughts, something else shifted in the air. I heard the faintest sound, a shuffle behind me. I spun around, heart hammering in my chest.

Nothing.

But the feeling—the one that had been creeping up on me for days—was now undeniable. I wasn't alone.

I had just uncovered something huge, but I wasn't sure if I'd live long enough to figure out what it meant.

Chapter 19

The days since Dad's arrest had been a blur. I couldn't shake the nagging feeling that I was missing something—something huge. My mind kept going back to the man in the trench coat, the one I'd seen when I was five, and then again just days ago, lurking in the shadows. Something about him didn't sit right.

I had started to believe he wasn't just some random figure haunting my past. No, he was connected to Uncle Martin's death.

The more I thought about it, the more sure I was that he was somehow involved in the mystery surrounding my uncle.

I decided it was time to dig deeper, to confront the facts head-on. I began to piece together everything I had learned so far: the journal, my dad's arrest, the whispers of hidden secrets. All the threads seemed to lead back to one thing: the murder of Uncle Martin. But who had really killed him? And why did Dad seem to be hiding so much?

I revisited the news articles about the robbery and looked up more about the unsolved cases, especially one that had been tied to my uncle's death. That's when I found it—an article buried deep in an obscure section of the local news archives.

"Detective Paul Harris Investigating Murder of Martin Westbrook."

I read the article twice, my pulse quickening. Detective Paul Harris? The man in the trench coat was a detective. He had been looking into Uncle Martin's death the entire time. And somehow, my dad had been involved, even though he was now in jail for a completely separate crime.

I felt the pieces finally start to click together.

The article detailed a cold case investigation into Uncle Martin's murder. It mentioned that the case had been reopened after new evidence had surfaced, but it didn't go into specifics. The detective, Harris, was the lead investigator, his number was on the website. And the more I read, the more connections I saw between him and the people I knew.

The article also mentioned a crucial detail—the night of Uncle Martin's death, a man had been seen leaving his house just moments before the police arrived. The man was never identified, but he was wearing a trench coat, and he had vanished without a trace.

I froze. The man in the trench coat wasn't some random stranger. He was the key to it all.

But there was more. I dug deeper into the case files, learning that Detective Harris had suspected a former associate of my father's—someone named Rick Donovan. The name struck me like a lightning bolt. Donovan was a name I'd heard whispered around the house when I was younger, but I hadn't thought much of it at the time.

Rick Donovan. He had been one of the people my dad and Uncle Martin worked with on... whatever it was they did. And according to the case file, he had been a prime suspect in the murder of Uncle Martin.

I couldn't believe it. All this time, I had thought my father might be hiding something, but it wasn't him who had killed Uncle Martin. It was Rick Donovan.

But why? Why had Donovan killed Uncle Martin, and why had my dad been involved?

I had to confront the truth. I had to find out everything.

It wasn't just the trench coat man that was trying to keep the truth hidden. It was Rick Donovan—and somehow, he was still out there, possibly even involved in my father's robbery. I had to find him, and had to figure out what really happened that night.

There was a sudden knock at my door, breaking me from my thoughts. My heart skipped a beat.

"Martin, we need to talk," my mom's voice called from the other side.

I quickly shoved the files back into my desk drawer and stood up. But I knew one thing for sure: the answers were closer than ever.

Chapter 20

The tension in the air felt heavier than it ever had before. I had finally put together the pieces: Rick Donovan was the person I had believed to be the killer of Uncle Martin. His name had been tied to everything—the unsolved murder, the shady business deals, and my father's involvement. And now, I was determined to confront him, to uncover the truth once and for all.

I had tracked Donovan's last known location, a small, run-down house on the outskirts of town. It looked abandoned, the paint peeling off the walls, the lawn unkempt. But something about the place seemed… off. As I stood there in front of the house, my heart pounded in my chest. What if he was still alive? What if I was finally about to confront the man responsible for Uncle Martin's death?

I hesitated before I pushed open the creaky gate and walked toward the house. Every step felt heavier, as though the earth itself was urging me to turn back. But I couldn't. I had to know.

I reached the front door and knocked three times, the sound echoing through the empty yard. There was no answer. I knocked again, this time harder, but still, no reply.

"Donovan," I muttered under my breath, my hands trembling with both fear and anger. "Where are you?"

I turned away from the door, scanning the perimeter of the house. That's when I saw it—an old, rusted sign nailed to the side of a fence that separated the yard from a small cemetery. My heart skipped a beat. It was barely legible, but there, in faded letters, was a name: *Rick Donovan*.

I froze. This couldn't be right. This couldn't be the same person. I had done my research. Donovan was supposed to be alive, or at least, he had been until recently. I followed the narrow path toward the graveyard, the hairs on the back of my neck standing up as I stepped past the weathered tombstones.

And then I saw it—Rick Donovan's gravestone.

The inscription was simple: *Rick Donovan, Beloved Father and Husband, 1975-2017*.

I felt my stomach drop. My hands went numb, and my mind raced. How could this be? The man I had been chasing, the person I thought was responsible for Uncle Martin's murder, had been dead for over two years. But the truth hit me like a ton of bricks: Donovan had died before my uncle. There was no way he could have killed Martin if he was already gone.

I stumbled back, my breath coming in shallow gasps. My entire world tilted, and for a moment, I couldn't process what I was seeing. This couldn't be happening. The killer—Donovan—wasn't alive anymore. I had been chasing shadows

Chapter 21

I stood frozen in front of the gravestone, my eyes unable to believe what they were seeing. The cold wind whipped through the cemetery, but I barely noticed it, my focus entirely consumed by the name carved into the stone.

Rick Donovan
October 15, 1981 – April 12, 2017

My heart skipped a beat. This couldn't be right. Rick Donovan, the man I had suspected to be my uncle Martin's killer, had died years ago—years before Uncle Martin was even murdered.

The realization hit me like a punch to the gut. I had been chasing the wrong person this entire time.

I stumbled back, feeling the ground spin beneath me. How could I have missed this? I had spent weeks connecting dots, investigating leads, and putting together a case against a man who had already been buried in the ground.

I looked down at the grave again, trying to process what this meant. If Donovan was dead before Uncle Martin, then someone else had to be the murderer. But who?

I turned around quickly, my mind reeling with questions. I couldn't stay here much longer. It was too much to take in. How had I gotten it so wrong? My hands were shaking as I pulled out my phone and called the only person who might have answers: Detective Harris.

The call rang through, and after a moment, the line clicked.

"Detective Harris," he answered.

"Detective, it's Martin," I said, trying to steady my voice. "I found something. Something big."

"What did you find, kid?" he asked, his voice calm but with a hint of curiosity.

"It's about Rick Donovan. He's dead. He died a couple of years ago, long before Uncle Martin was killed. I was chasing the wrong lead. That means… the killer has to be someone else."

There was a long pause on the other end of the line, and then Harris spoke, his tone grave.

"I've suspected for a while that Donovan wasn't the one who did it. But there's something else you need to know, Martin."

"What is it?" I asked, the desperation in my voice growing.

"The investigation into your uncle's death, the real one—well, it was never closed. We may have thought we knew who did it, but the case is still open. And the real killer? He's much closer to you than you think."

I felt a chill run down my spine. My mind raced, trying to process what he was saying.

"Closer to me? Who?" I demanded, feeling my heart beat faster with every passing second.

"Look inside your own family. Sometimes, the answers you're looking for are closer than you realize."

The line went dead before I could respond, and I stood there, frozen in the cemetery, my mind swirling with this new revelation. The killer wasn't who I thought. It wasn't Rick Donovan.

The truth was much darker, and it was closer to home than I ever could have imagined.

I turned back toward the gravestone, staring at the name of the man who had once seemed like the answer. Rick Donovan may have been dead, but the real story was far from over.

As I walked away from the grave, the fog growing thicker around me, I couldn't shake the feeling that the next truth I uncovered would change everything.

Chapter 22

The final piece

The house was unnervingly silent that night, the kind of silence that pressed on my ears and made my thoughts seem deafening. I couldn't shake Detective Harris's words: *"Look inside your own family."*

I hadn't told anyone about what I'd found at Rick Donovan's grave. I couldn't. If the killer was closer than I realized, how close were we talking? Every interaction I'd had over the past few days replayed in my mind. My dad's arrest, Max's innocence, my mother's composed demeanor—it all felt like puzzle pieces that didn't fit.

The only place left to search was my parents' bedroom, the one room in the house I'd always been told to stay out of.

I waited until late, until I was sure Max was asleep and the faint sound of my mother's TV shows in the living room echoed softly through the house. Heart pounding, I crept upstairs, avoiding the one squeaky floorboard by the landing.

The door to my parents' bedroom creaked as I pushed it open, and I froze, holding my breath. Nothing stirred. I slipped inside, carefully closing the door behind me.

The room was unnaturally neat—too neat, considering my dad hadn't been home for weeks. His side of the bed was untouched, his things neatly packed away as if he were nothing more than a guest.

I started with the dresser, rifling through drawers filled with socks, shirts, and old photographs. Nothing. Next, I checked the closet. Rows of my mom's blouses hung neatly alongside a small collection of my dad's jackets. My fingers brushed the back of the closet, searching for any hidden compartments or loose panels. Still nothing.

Frustration bubbled in my chest. What was I even looking for?

Then my foot caught on something—the edge of a rug. I glanced down and saw the corner was slightly lifted. I knelt and pulled it back, revealing a wooden floorboard with faint scratches around its edges.

My heart raced as I dug my fingers into the grooves, prying it up. Beneath the board was a small, dark opening.

A hidden room.

I stared at it, disbelief washing over me. Why would my parents have a secret room?

I grabbed my phone, turned on the flashlight, and lowered myself through the opening. The hidden space smelled of dust and time, the air thick and stale. My flashlight illuminated shelves of boxes and papers stacked haphazardly.

And there, hanging on a hook on the far wall, was the trench coat.

The same trench coat I'd seen when I was five.

Beside it, a matching hat sat neatly on a shelf.

My breath caught in my throat as memories from years ago rushed back—seeing the man in the trench coat on the night Uncle Martin died, watching him vanish into the darkness. But this couldn't be real. Why would the coat and hat be here, in my parents' hidden room?

I stepped closer, my hands trembling as I reached for a nearby box. The lid came off easily, revealing a collection of documents and photos.

One photo made my stomach drop: it was a picture of my mom and Uncle Martin, taken years before I was born. They were smiling, but the look in my mom's eyes wasn't one of happiness—it was something darker.

Underneath the photo were letters. Dozens of them. As I flipped through them, the story began to unfold.

Uncle Martin had been blackmailing my mom. The letters detailed threats to reveal some kind of "past" that my mom had desperately tried to bury.

One letter in particular made my blood run cold:

"You think you can just walk away from everything, Cali? From me? I know what you did. And if you don't pay up, the whole family will know too."

The signature was unmistakable: Uncle Martin.

I stumbled back, piecing it all together. My mom had killed Uncle Martin. The man in the trench coat wasn't some ominous figure haunting my past—it had been my mom all along.

But why?

As I dug deeper into the boxes, the truth became clear. My mom's past wasn't just messy—it was criminal. She and Uncle Martin had been involved in illegal activities when they were younger. When she met my dad and started a family, she tried to leave it all behind, but Uncle Martin wouldn't let her.

She must have snapped.

The pieces fit together like a horrifying puzzle. Uncle Martin had threatened to ruin her, and she'd done the unthinkable to protect her new life.

I sat there in the hidden room, my mind spinning. All these years, I'd thought my family was just another suburban household with its quirks and secrets. But this—this was something else entirely.

A creak from upstairs snapped me out of my thoughts.

I scrambled to replace everything as I'd found it, shoving the boxes back and climbing out of the hidden room. I dropped the floorboard into place and pulled the rug over it just as the bedroom door opened.

My mom stood in the doorway, her face shadowed in the dim light.

"What are you doing here, Martin?" she asked, her voice calm but laced with an edge.

I tried to think of an excuse, but the words wouldn't come.

"I know," I said finally, my voice barely above a whisper.

Her expression didn't change. "Know what?"

"About Uncle Martin. About the letters. About the trench coat."

She stepped into the room, closing the door behind her. "You don't understand, Martin," she said, her tone softening. "I did what I had to do to protect this family."

"Protect us? You killed him!" I said, my voice breaking. "How could you?"

Tears welled in her eyes, but she didn't deny it. "You don't know what he was capable of. What he would have done to us if I hadn't—"

"I don't care what he would've done!" I shouted. "You lied to us. You let us live with this lie for years!"

She took a step closer, her hands trembling. "Martin, I did it for you. For Max. For your father. Everything I've ever done was to keep this family safe."

I shook my head, backing away. "You didn't do this for us. You did it for yourself."

The weight of her betrayal was crushing. Everything I thought I knew about my family was a lie.

"I'm calling Detective Harris," I said, my voice steadier now. "You have to turn yourself in."

Her face crumpled, and for a moment, I saw the mother I'd always known—the one who cared for us, who loved us. But now, that image was shattered.

As I walked out of the room, I knew my life would never be the same.The truth was out. And it had destroyed everything.

Chapter 23

Aftermath

The house felt different after that night—quieter, emptier, like it had lost something vital. The truth had cracked its foundation, leaving nothing but fractured pieces that I wasn't sure could ever be put back together.

Detective Harris had arrived shortly after my call. I had expected anger, yelling, maybe even tears from my mom, but she had been eerily calm. She didn't deny anything. She simply sat in the living room, her hands folded in her lap, as if she'd been expecting this moment all along.

The memory of her being led away in handcuffs would haunt me forever. She didn't look back at me or Max. Maybe she couldn't bear to. Or maybe she thought she didn't deserve to.

Now it was just me, Max, and the shadow of what used to be our family.

Max didn't fully understand what had happened. I tried to shield him from the worst of it, but the absence of our mom was impossible to ignore.

"Where's Mom?" he asked one morning at breakfast, his wide, innocent eyes staring up at me.

"She's… away," I said, fumbling for the right words. "She had to go take care of something really important."

"When is she coming back?"

I hesitated, my throat tightening. "I don't know, Max."

He didn't ask any more questions, but I could see the confusion and sadness in his face. He clung to me more than ever, his stuffed dinosaur always in hand. I tried to be strong for him, but inside, I was crumbling.

A week after my mom's arrest, I went to visit my dad in jail. He'd been awaiting trial for the bank robbery, and I hadn't seen him since the night everything unraveled.

When I sat down in the cold, sterile visiting room, he looked older—tired, defeated.

"Martin," he said, his voice heavy. "I heard about your mother."

I nodded, not trusting myself to speak.

"She… she told me everything during her visit," he continued, rubbing his hands together. "I didn't know, Martin. I swear to you, I had no idea what she'd done."

"Didn't you?" I asked, my voice sharper than I intended. "She had a hidden room in your bedroom. You didn't notice anything?"

His eyes dropped to the table. "I knew she was keeping secrets, but I thought they were from before we met. I never imagined…" He trailed off, shaking his head. "I thought she'd left that life behind."

The anger I'd been holding back finally bubbled to the surface. "She killed Uncle Martin! She lied to us for years, and you just… let it happen!"

"I didn't *let* anything happen!" he snapped, his voice rising. "Do you think I wanted this? Do you think I wanted any of this for our family?"

Silence stretched between us, heavy and suffocating.

"I'm sorry," he said finally, his voice breaking. "For everything. For what I did, for what your mom did. We've failed you, Martin. Both of us."

I didn't respond. What could I say?

With both my parents gone, my grandparents stepped in to take care of Max and me. They moved into the house, trying to create some semblance of normalcy.

But nothing felt normal anymore.

At night, I lay awake replaying everything that had happened—the secrets, the lies, the betrayals. I thought about Uncle Martin, about what kind of man he'd really been. He wasn't the saint my mother had made him out to be, but he didn't deserve what happened to him.

And then there was my mom. I wanted to hate her. Part of me did. But another part of me—the part that remembered her singing lullabies to Max, baking cookies with me, and always being there when I needed her—still loved her.

How could I reconcile the woman who raised me with the woman who'd taken a life?

Detective Harris visited a few weeks later to check on me.

"You did the right thing," he said, sitting across from me at the kitchen table.

"Did I?" I asked, staring at my hands. "Everything's worse now. My family's gone, and Max… he doesn't even know the truth. How is any of this the 'right thing'?"

Harris sighed, leaning back in his chair. "The truth is messy, Martin. It doesn't always fix things. But it's better than living a lie."

I wanted to believe him. But as I looked around the empty house, the walls echoing with memories that felt like they belonged to someone else, I wasn't so sure.

Months passed. Life went on, though it didn't feel like it at first. Max started to adjust, and I threw myself into school and helped around the house.

One day, while cleaning out the hidden room in my parents' bedroom, I found a note tucked inside a book. It was addressed to me in my mother's handwriting.

Martin,

By the time you read this, you'll know the truth. I wish I could explain everything, but there are things I can never make right. All I can say is that I'm sorry—for the lies, for the pain, for the choices I made. I hope one day you can forgive me. Take care of Max. He needs you now more than ever.

Love, Mom

Tears blurred my vision as I folded the note and put it back in the book. Forgiveness would take time—maybe a lifetime. But for Max's sake, I had to try.

As I looked around the house, I realized it wasn't just the secrets that had shattered our family—it was the silence. And if I was going to move forward, I couldn't let silence win.

This was our home, our life. And I was determined to rebuild it, one piece at a time.

With both my parents gone, my grandparents stepped in to take care of Max and me. They moved into the house, trying to create some semblance of normalcy.

But nothing felt normal anymore.

At night, I lay awake replaying everything that had happened—the secrets, the lies, the betrayals. I thought about Uncle Martin, about what kind of man he'd really been. He wasn't the saint my mother had made him out to be, but he didn't deserve what happened to him.

And then there was my mom. I wanted to hate her. Part of me did. But another part of me—the part that remembered her singing lullabies to Max, baking cookies with me, and always being there when I needed her—still loved her.

How could I reconcile the woman who raised me with the woman who'd taken a life?

Detective Harris visited a few weeks later to check on me.

"You did the right thing," he said, sitting across from me at the kitchen table.

"Did I?" I asked, staring at my hands. "Everything's worse now. My family's gone, and Max… he doesn't even know the truth. How is any of this the 'right thing'?"

Harris sighed, leaning back in his chair. "The truth is messy, Martin. It doesn't always fix things. But it's better than living a lie."

I wanted to believe him. But as I looked around the empty house, the walls echoing with memories that felt like they belonged to someone else, I wasn't so sure.

Months passed. Life went on, though it didn't feel like it at first. Max started to adjust, and I threw myself into school and helping around the house.

THE END

Chapter 24

The final thread

Life was slowly settling into a new normal—or as close to normal as it could get. Max was doing better, and I was finding ways to keep myself busy. But late at night, when the house was quiet, I couldn't shake the feeling that there were still pieces of the puzzle

there was my dad's job—the mystery he had guarded so fiercely. Even with everything I'd uncovered, that question remained unanswered.

It was late one night when I found myself back in the study. I wasn't looking for anything in particular, just wandering through the remnants of the life we'd left behind. That's when I noticed a loose floorboard near the desk—something I'd somehow missed before.

Curiosity prickled at me as I pried it up. Beneath it was a small metal box, the kind with a combination lock. I carried it to the desk and tried a few guesses. After several failed attempts, I realized it was my dad's birthday. The lock clicked open.

Inside was a stack of papers, a set of photographs, and an ID badge.

I picked up the badge first. My dad's picture stared back at me, but the name on it wasn't his. It read: **Special Agent Carter Hall, Federal Bureau of Investigation.**

I blinked, the pieces clicking into place. My dad wasn't just working a secret job—he'd been an FBI agent.

The photographs were next. They were grainy surveillance images of a man in a trench coat—always the same man, always watching. My pulse quickened as I flipped through them, each one dated and marked with locations.

The last photograph wasn't a surveillance shot. It was a candid picture of my dad and the man in the trench coat, standing together outside a diner. They weren't arguing or looking suspicious—they were smiling, shaking hands.

"What the…?" I muttered, staring at the image.

Beneath the photos was a file folder labeled: *Operation Crossroads.*

So I was wrong about my mom being the man in the trench coat?.

The file contained pages of cryptic notes, timelines, and maps. My dad had been investigating a massive criminal network tied to several unsolved murders—including my Uncle Martin's.

One note caught my eye. It was handwritten in my dad's messy scrawl:

Suspect eliminated. Internal connections remain. Proceed with caution.

Eliminated? Did that mean… My dad had killed someone? Or did it mean someone else had?

Another page listed names, and my uncle's name was circled in red. Next to it was written: *Informant?*

My mind reeled. Uncle Martin wasn't just a victim—he might've been involved in something dangerous, maybe even working with my dad.

The sound of my phone buzzing snapped me out of my thoughts. I didn't recognize the number, but I answered anyway.

"Hello?"

"Martin." The voice was deep and unfamiliar.

"Who is this?"

"Someone who knows you've been digging where you don't belong."

My blood ran cold. "What do you want?"

"I want you to stop asking questions. Your father and your uncle were part of something bigger than you can understand. Let it go, or you'll end up like them."

The line went dead.

Shaking, I looked back at the box. At the bottom was one final item—a key, attached to a tag that read: *Locker 13.*

I didn't know what the key would open or where it would lead, but one thing was clear: the story wasn't over.

As I sat in the dim study, the weight of everything pressed down on me. My dad, the trench coat man, my uncle—every thread was leading somewhere.

And I was determined to follow it, no matter where it took me.

TO BE Continued